Workbook: **English**

Afsaneh

One from Many

یکی از همه

افسانه

This booklet belongs to:

_____

_____

_____

_____

_____

_____

Köln © 2024   Vera Ansén

Bibliografische Information der Deutschen Nationalbibliothek: Die Deutsche Nationalbibliothek verzeichnet diese Publikation in der Deutschen Nationalbibliografie; detaillierte bibliografische Daten sind im Internet über dnb.dnb.de abrufbar.

First Edition
© 2024 Vera Ansén

Idee, Text & Grafik: Vera Ansén
Satz & Layout: Ansén & Ansén
Lektorat: Rebecca Ansén

Verlag: BoD · Books on Demand GmbH, In de Tarpen 42, 22848 Norderstedt
Druck: Libri Plureos GmbH, Friedensallee 273, 22763 Hamburg

ISBN: 978-3-7693-2048-0

Contents:

Welcome to Your Quest!

This workbook guides you through the stories and themes of *Afsaneh – One from Many*. It helps you explore the cultural and historical facets of Iran while encouraging you to reflect on your own thoughts and develop an independent perspective.

Afsaneh's stories are filled with warmth and pride, shaped by her deep connection to her home country. Yet, they also reflect her uniquely personal view of the world.
This workbook invites you to look beyond her stories:
What do these experiences mean to you?
What questions do they spark, and what answers can you find for yourself?

The subtitle, "What was Iran?", captures the essence: It is not just about understanding a country's past but also about reflecting on what it means for the present and future.
Rather than ready-made answers, this workbook focuses on questions:

- What shapes a culture?
- How do personal experiences influence our perspectives?
- What can we learn from this for our own lives?

Your stake:

- Look closely! Discover details, recognize patterns, and understand connections.
- Reflect! What do Afsaneh's experiences mean to you personally?
- Deepen your knowledge! Review what you have learned and use creative tasks to discover new insights.

Why this workbook is different:

This workbook equips you with tools to think independently and critically. It challenges you not just to learn facts but to contextualize them and connect them to your own world.

As Afsaneh says:
"Treating the past as a vision of the future only leads to confusion. We can only truly meet each other in the 'here and now'"

This workbook helps you:

- Learn more about Iran, its history, and its culture.
- Understand and question different perspectives.
- Develop your own opinions – free from prejudice.

You are the creator of your insights. And who knows?
You might discover answers to questions you have not even thought to ask yet.

Our thoughts are free – let's begin!

Here we go!

Her Invitation

The following section I is designed to guide your exploration of pages 7-17

of   Afsaneh – One from Many

The next pages allow you to dive into the following topics:

My beloved sister,

it has been a long time since the same fire brightened our faces. I miss your eyes alight as we listened to the stories of the elders, and your laughter that so beautifully awakened my senses.

When I hear the birds in the early morning, chirping and singing with joy to greet the new day, their untamed zest for life fills me. I remember how we spread our arms and ran wildly around. Enchanted by the thought that if only we were light enough, we could fly like the birds, so endlessly free. The world was our home. We knew no boundaries, no obligations, no laws — only the love of our mother and her sometimes stern gaze that made us pause when we were too wild.

The moment we held our own children in our arms, whom we wanted to love and protect, that lightness of those days was gone.

As our mother, full of wonder, first looked into our eyes. Full of curiosity about what we might bring into her life. She knew we would not be like our siblings, that a different fate awaited us. That each child finds its own melody and its very own journey through life. All we can offer is loving encouragement toward good thoughts, good words, and good deeds.

None of us endured the hours of birth just to lose this life to any war, not to hatred among siblings, not to the battles of men, not to the interests of power. To fight in the name of love requires entirely different means than those others want to impose on us!

We have become strangers, yet our hearts and feelings must not grow cold.

It does not matter to me whether we were born of the same womb or are related by blood. This book carries the experiences of thousands of women.

Women who, like me, were on the verge of being uprooted and had to find their place in life through tears! Home — let me tell you this — is only known to those in exile; all others are simply at home! Today, my home is Germany, but in my heart, I will forever be a Persian who painfully misses her homeland.

"Well, you must be glad to be here now..." is the most heartless question one can ask me. That is why I want you to know everything about me and see yourself in my story!

Faithfully yours

Afsaneh

- What is the purpose of starting the book with a letter?
- Who is the sender, and who is the recipient?
- What is your first impression upon reading Afsaneh's letter?
- Which parts or sentences resonate with you the most? Highlight them in the text!

Cultural Connection:

• What similarities or differences between Afsaneh's world and your own stand out to you?

Decoding Quotes and Metaphors:

• What do the chosen images or sayings in the letter mean?

• Why do you think Afsaneh chose these particular words?

A) The Letter: Introduction and Intercultural Reflection

Self-Reflection:

• What thoughts or questions came to your mind after reading the letter?

Reflect separately.

To Do:

1. Read Aloud:

• Read Afsaneh's letter aloud in small groups.

• Discuss together: Which parts should be emphasized?

• Why?

2. Create a Voice Message:

• Imagine you need to record Afsaneh's letter as a voice message or audio clip.

• Record the text in a way that conveys the emotions behind Afsaneh's words to the listener.

3. Thoughts in the Letter:

• Which ideas or words in the letter stand out as particularly important?

• Do you think these ideas are as relevant to your life today as they were in Afsaneh's time?

Vocabulary Bank

• Look for words in the letter you don't know.

• Add these words to your vocabulary bank.

• Write down their meanings and reflect: Which of these words could you use in your daily life?

B) Woman - Life - Freedom

Reflection:
- What do the three words
Woman - Life - Freedom
mean to you?

- Think about your own environment: Which rights or freedoms do you take for granted that others may not have?

Reflect separately.

Check the Background:

- Where does the slogan *Woman - Life - Freedom* originate from?
- Who coined it, and why?
- What kinds of people are involved, and what are they trying to achieve?

- What might these words mean to people living under challenging political or societal conditions?

- Why is this slogan significant not only for women but also for men and children?

B) *Woman - Life - Freedom:* A Global Movement

• What connections can you identify between the struggles for freedom and equality in other parts of the world?

• What does the demand *"Keep state out of women's lives!"* mean to you?

To Do:

1. Online Research:

• Search for recent articles, videos, or reports about the *Woman - Life - Freedom* movement.

• Present three key points that surprised or impressed you and explain why.

2. Group Discussion:

• Exchange ideas in small groups.

• Discuss: Why are not only women but also men and others involved in this movement?

3. Creative Task:

• If you were to design a poster or a social media message to invite others to engage with *Woman - Life - Freedom*, how would you make your message short and easy to understand?

Vocabulary Bank

• Note down words or terms you didn't understand during your research and add them to your Vocabulary Bank.

  • Write down their meanings and discuss: Why are these terms essential for understanding the movement?

☐
☐
☐
☐
☐
☐
☐
☐

C) Iran and the United Nations

Reflection:

• Did you know that Iran was one of the founding members of the United Nations (UN)?

• What does it mean for a country to be part of establishing an organization dedicated to global peace and cooperation?

Check the Background:
- When were the United Nations founded, and why?
- What role did Iran play in the founding of the UN?

• After World War II, Soviet troops stayed longer than agreed in Iran. Iran brought this issue before the UN Security Council. What resolutions were passed in this context?

• Why were these resolutions important at the time, and what significance might they still hold today?

• Are there similar issues today that you consider important for the UN's work?

Reflect separately.

Cultural Connection:

• What connections can you identify between the UN's work and the values of *Woman - Life - Freedom* from point B?

• What does Iran's active role in founding the UN reveal about its position in the global community at that time?

Self-Reflection:

 • Reflect on this: How can a single country contribute to solving global problems through the United Nations?

_____

_____

_____

_____

_____

_____

_____

_____

_____

_____

_____

_____

_____

• Brainstorm and collect your ideas: What issues would you bring to the UN if you were representing a country?

_____

_____

_____

_____

_____

_____

To Do:

1. Group Discussion:
• Exchange ideas in small groups.
• Discuss: Why is it important for countries like Iran to actively participate in international organizations?
• Consider together: What challenges might a country like Iran face in being heard at the UN?

2. Creative Task:
• Imagine you are delegates of Iran in 1946. Draft a speech explaining why the withdrawal of Soviet troops is crucial.

• You can present the speech to your group or write it as a text.

Vocabulary Bank
• Note down words or terms you didn't understand during your research and add them to your Vocabulary Bank.
• Write down their meanings and discuss how these terms relate to the UN and Iran?

☐
☐
☐
☐
☐
☐
☐
☐

D) Rumi – The Persian Poet and Philosopher

- How familiar were you with Rumi before reading *Afsaneh*?
- Which of his verses did you already know?

- Who was Rumi?
What do you discover about him?
- Why is Rumi, a 13th-century poet, still renowned and appreciated worldwide today?
- Are there modern artists or public figures who draw inspiration from him?

- Rumi spoke about universal values like love, patience, and inner growth. Does his famous quote, "Beyond right and wrong, there is a field. I'll meet you there," still fit in today's world?

Self-Reflection:

- Rumi was forced to flee the city where he lived. Who might have offered him refuge?

_____

_____

_____

_____

_____

_____

_____

_____

- Which experience from your own life would you like to share with Rumi?

_____

_____

_____

_____

_____

_____

_____

_____

 • Would Rumi have been an ally of the *Woman - Life - Freedom* movement? Discuss why?

• Which of Rumi's ideas align with what we've learned in previous chapters about *Woman - Life - Freedom*?

Your
favorite Verse

To Do:

1. Read Aloud and Discuss:
• Read Rumi quotes from the text aloud and discuss in class what they might mean.
• Which messages resonate with you the most? Why?

2. Creative Task:
• Write a short poem or reflection inspired by one of Rumi's quotes. You can also choose a verse you find online.

• How might Rumi describe a modern conflict?
Write a brief message in Rumi's style.

• Why are his messages about love and humanity still relevant today?

_____

_____

Reflect separately.

Vocabulary Bank
• Collect unfamiliar terms you find in Rumi's quotes or background story.
• Add these to your Vocabulary Bank and include their definitions!

☐
☐
☐
☐
☐
☐

My
Notes

The following section II guides your exploration
of pages 18-27

of   Afsaneh ~ One from Many

The next pages allow you to dive into the following topics:

As a sturdy, blonde girl, I started asking myself early on which chords the Nazis might have struck in me if I had been born in 1927 instead of 1972?

Not exactly by choice, as I remembered while writing down these notes: In our high school, we had a traveling exhibition on the extermination in the concentration camps between 1936 and 1945. Faced with countless photos of mutilated and buried bodies of the dead, I couldn't hold back my tears. A chubby, dark-haired classmate responded to me:

"Why are you even crying? With those blue eyes of yours, you wouldn't have had anything to fear under the Nazis!"

With his words, which held as much insight as fear, he mocked my compassion. Words that struck me deeply. Neither my country of birth, nor my era, nor my appearance were a choice of my own.

Would I have held any power as a 12-year-old in that dreadful time?

How does one confront villains who present their own well-being as the welfare of the people, their own profit as national progress? Who invoke nation, though the lives and freedom of their compatriots mean nothing to them? How does one handle the responsibility of not becoming the target of persecution or discrimination oneself?

How to resist the temptation — to elevate oneself above others when circumstances allow — is a question that troubles people worldwide.

A) Youth under Fascism: Responsibility and Compassion

2. My Notes - Section II .... Pages 18-27

- What might it mean to grow up as a teenager during the Nazi era?
- How might one have acted in a time when conformity and resistance could mean the difference between life and death?

- Is a lack of knowledge an excuse for actions or inaction?

Reflect separately.

- Can young people be held accountable for their decisions under totalitarian regimes?

PROS	CONS

- What could help young people today avoid making the same mistakes?

1. Group Discussion:
• Discuss how you think you would have felt
in such a situation.
• What decisions would you have made as a 15-year-old?
Share your thoughts honestly and provide reasons for your
views.

2. Creative Task:
• Write a diary entry from the perspective of a 15-year-old
in Germany 1942.
• Consider the daily life, fears, and possible decisions they
might face.

A) Youth under Fascism: Responsibility and Compassion

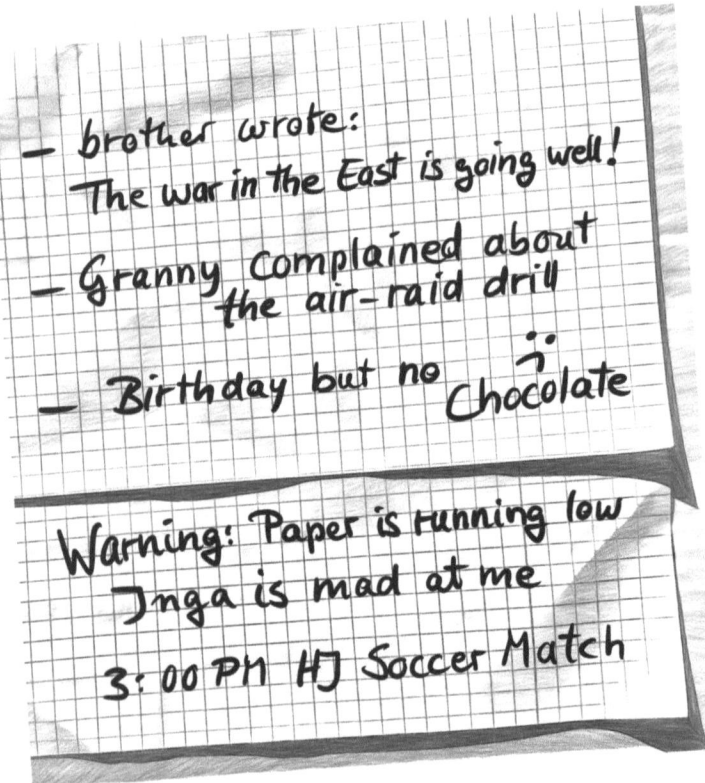

— brother wrote:
The war in the East is going well!

— Granny complained about
the air-raid drill

— Birthday but no Chocolate :)

Warning: Paper is running low
Inga is mad at me
3:00 PM HJ Soccer Match

Check the Background:

- **Comparison with other Dictatorships:** Research examples from other countries and times where youth were confronted with fascist or authoritarian systems.
- **Parallels and Differences:** How similar or different were these experiences compared to Nazi Germany?

"If I had been born in 1927 instead of 1972 ..."

- What thoughts does this consideration spark in you? Reason why it might be important to reflect on this past over and over again.

Reflect separately.

Vocabulary Bank
- Note terms such as: fascism, conformism, resistance, propaganda, responsibility.
- Add additional terms discovered during your research and define them together in your Vocabulary Bank.

☐
☐
☐
☐
☐
☐
☐
☐

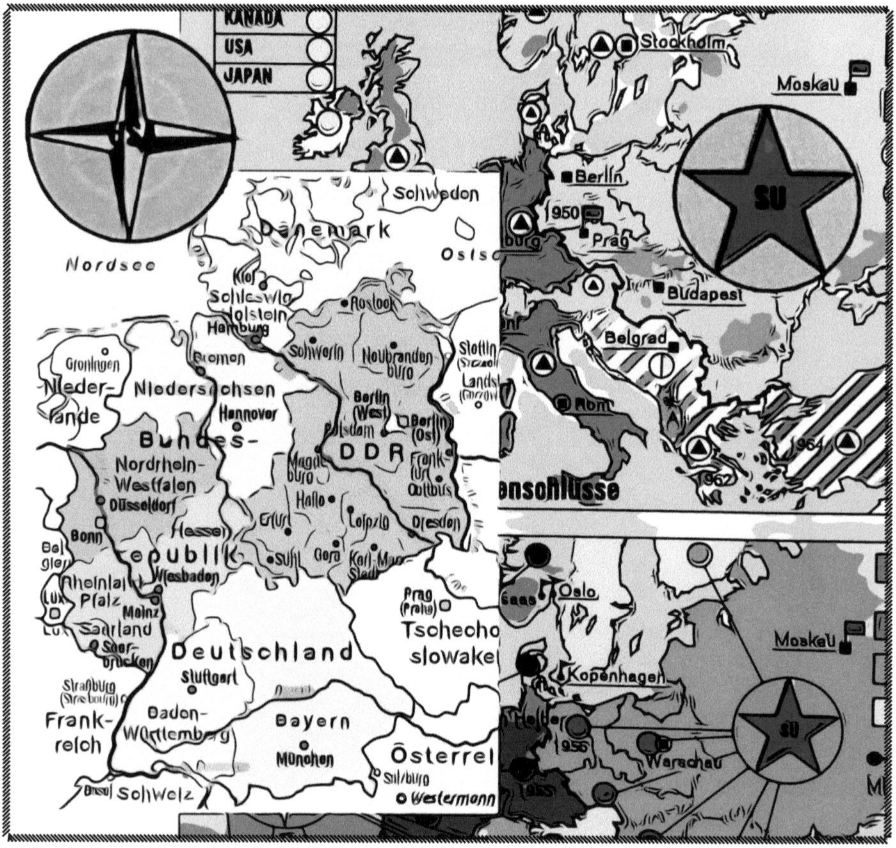

• What do boundaries mean in your life – physical, social, or cultural?

• Why do people create boundaries, and what happens when these boundaries shift?

• Are boundaries a form of protection or an obstacle?

Reflect separately.

- Are boundaries always fixed, or can they be invisible and fluid?
- What happens when boundaries are not respected – for individuals and for societies?

FOR INDIVIDUALS	FOR A COMMUNITY

Check the Background:

- How do medieval city societies differ from modern nation-states?
- Research examples of boundary formations in history, such as city walls, colonial borders, or the Berlin Wall.
- Analyze the statement: "Borders make it much easier to create enforceable legal systems."

- Since when have nation-states existed?

Reflect separately.

To Do:

1. Group Discussion:
• How can boundaries connect or divide people?
• Take a class poll: Are boundaries more of a protection or a barrier?

2. Creative Task:
• Draw a map of your ideal city.
• Think about neighborhoods, community spaces, and boundaries. Should these be open or closed?
• Imagine you need to restrict access to certain areas of the city to prevent a threat (e.g. flooding, spread of a pandemic). How would you approach this?

Document measures and methods:

• Which safety measures were agreed upon as acceptable:

• What kinds of people would you need to ensure the safety of a city with a large population?

B) Boundaries: Urban Societies and Nations

Self-Reflection:

- Are there boundaries in your life that are not visible but still affect you?

Vocabulary Bank
- Note down terms such as: urban society, nation, boundary, legal system, connection, separation.
  - Add more terms and list examples of historical or cultural boundaries.

☐
☐
☐
☐
☐
☐
☐
☐

"You, woman!" was a teasing term of endearment among us girls in my youth, as we dealt with our first menstrual discomforts. It was our way of parodying gender labels that we no longer felt applied to us.

Feminism was yesterday? We thought the world was ours!

Language has power. It can comfort, motivate, and connect, but it can also exclude, dehumanize, and oppress.
• How does language shape our thinking and actions?

• Write a sentence of brave words that inspires you to stand up for your beliefs with confidence.

Reflect separately.

1. Group Discussion:
• Find examples where language in your daily life or in the media uplifts or degrades people.
• How does language shape our thinking and actions?
• Why is language often used on purpose to discriminate against certain groups?

2. Creative Task:
• Create a "message of joy" that everyone should hear.
• What would you say, and why?
• Write this message on a large poster and design it together as a group.

Check the Background:

- How does the Iranian state respond to young women who refuse to wear a headscarf in 2024?
- What impact does the term "mentally ill" have on people, the society, and the person affected who hears it?

Self-Reflection:

- Which words in the schoolyard make you keep your distance from classmates?

Vocabulary Bank

- Note down words that become important during the discussion: empathy, resistance, discrimination, stigmatization, feminism.
  - Add more terms to your Vocabulary Bank as they come up.

☐

☐

☐

☐

☐

☐

☐

☐

D) Prosperity through Sustainable Management

How Iran nourished people over millennia

Check the Background:

- Research the significance of Iran in the history of agriculture. What innovations, such as qanats or irrigation systems, were developed there, and during which periods?
- Investigate how these technologies impacted the quality of life for people: Why are these technologies considered sustainable?

- Investigate how different population groups – from nomads to city dwellers – benefited from the wealth of the region.

- What has research in anthropology and ancient Iranian studies revealed about the lifestyles and adaptability of people in this region?

1. Group Discussion:
- Why is it still important nowadays to use resources sustainably?
- Compare the ancient technologies of Iran with modern approaches to resource management, and think about what we can learn from ancient cultures today.

2. Creative Task:
- Create a map that illustrates how Iran functioned as a center of sustainable resource management. Highlight key resources such as water, fertile plains, and trade routes.

Self-Reflection:

• What measures allow for the peaceful coexistence of many people?

Describe how Iran could be a livable place for you, based on what you've learned about its geographical location, climate, and the wise use of natural resources over centuries.

_____

_____

_____

_____

_____

_____

_____

_____

Vocabulary Bank

• Add the terms sustainability, qanats, anthropology, ancient Iranian studies, irrigation systems, and other important words.

• Add more terms to your Vocabulary Bank as they come up.

☐
☐
☐
☐
☐
☐
☐
☐

Our
Dialogue

The following section III-IV guides your exploration of pages 28-75

of

Afsaneh ~ One from Many

The next pages allow you to dive into the following topics:

Afsaneh: *Did you know that the Iranian parliament passed a law in 1963 to establish the 'Army of Knowledge', which was awarded the UNESCO Education Prize in 1972?*

Check the Background:

- Find out what the "Army of Knowledge" was. How did it work, and what were its goals?
- What role did young teachers and educators play when they were sent to rural regions?

- Given that education is a human right, what responsibility does a state have to ensure this right is upheld?

Reflect separately.

1. Discuss:
- Why did the Shah emphasize education as a key part of his "White Revolution"?
- Compare the "Army of Knowledge" with modern educational initiatives in regions with structural challenges. What are the similarities and differences?

2. Creative Task:
- Imagine you are part of the "Army of Knowledge" and are writing a letter home describing your daily life in a remote village. What are the challenges and successes of your work?

3. Our Dialogue - Section III-IV .... Pages 28-75

Self-Reflection:

• Why does a lack of education hinder societal development and unity among people within a state?

Vocabulary Bank

• Add terms like literacy, Army of Knowledge, right to education, human rights, and equal opportunities.

• Discuss their meanings and add them to your Vocabulary Bank.

☐
☐
☐
☐
☐
☐
☐
☐

B) Fairy Tales: Tales that Travel

A king was blessed with the birth of a daughter, the most beautiful child he had ever seen. Then, a traveling dervish warned him that one day she would marry the son of his arch-enemy.

Many nights, the king lay sleepless, until one night a mighty phoenix landed on his balcony.

"Why do you grieve, wise king?" spoke the bird with shimmering feathers. "Hasn't the most beautiful girl, you have ever seen, been born to you?"

The king trusted the phoenix, so he confessed that he was tormented by the fear that the girl would be corrupted. Blinded by the radiant feathers of the magical bird, the king pleaded. "Oh, Phoenix, if a mighty being like you would protect my daughter, nothing bad could ever happen to her."

The bird promised the king to always take good care of the child and took her with him.

 • How would the fairy tale have ended if you had told it?

Check the Background:

- Find out which fairy tales are considered "typically German" but actually originate from stories in other cultures.
- Research how fairy tales were altered through oral storytelling or written collections like those of the Brothers Grimm.
- What were their origins?

Reflection:

- What similarities can be found between fairy tales from different parts of the world?

- Why do people tell stories, and how do they help connect cultures?

 Many fairy tales considered 'national' often originate from stories of other cultures.

• Compare a fairy tale from Europe with one from Iran. Which themes, characters, or motifs are repeated?

• What challenges and values are similarly depicted (e.g. greed, deceit, the quest for justice, outwitting a powerful adversary)?

1. Discuss:

• Why are fairy tales an important part of cultural identity, and how do they help us reflect on similarities between cultures?

• Think about how fairy tales can contribute to mutual understanding.

2. Creative Task:

• Ask your teacher to use maps or timelines to show the journey of fairy tales.

• Choose a fairy tale and illustrate how it traveled around the world.

 **Cultural Connection:**
- Choose a well-known story from your region or culture.
- Imagine it being told during a journey to another country.
- How might it change to be understood or appreciated in the new culture?

_____

_____

_____

_____

_____

_____

_____

_____

_____

_____

_____

Vocabulary Bank
- You can include terms like research on fairy tales, cultural connection, motifs, oral tradition, and adaptations.

☐

☐

☐

☐

☐

☐

C) Farah Diba:
Between Hard Work and Representation

- How could an influencer like Farah Diba shape perceptions of Iran and its culture, both then and now?

Check the Background:

- Look up information about Farah Diba's work for education, art, and women's rights.

Examples: Her support for the Tehran Museum of Contemporary Art or her role in opening the international UN Women's Conference in 1965

- Be creative: Imagine how Farah Diba might present herself on platforms like Instagram or TikTok in today's digital world.

Reflect separately.

Reflection:

• What qualities do people expect from a modern monarch? How does this image differ from that of a traditional fairy-tale princess?

• How did Farah Diba use her position to represent Iran on the international stage and inspire societal change?

1. First Impression:

• Consider Farah Diba in the context of a constitutional monarchy. How is her role comparable to monarchs in European countries such as Britain or the Netherlands?

2. Discuss:

• Why might she be described as an influencer of her time?

• In what ways could she serve as a role model for others?

D) "Unriddle the Comic": Power and Intrigue

The scandalously cruel story of Power in Persia as ISNOGUD might tell us*

*out of GOSCINNY's world

PREVIOUSLY IN PERSIA

Mohammad had a great-grandfather who sought ...

alleviation

ABBAS MIRZA FANCIED THE EUROPEAN STYLE

His heir* had the Prime Minister suffocated in a carpet.

*PROMISE KEPT: "NO BLOODSHED"!

His heir preferred a happy, poor folk to industrialzation that would bring misery.

? NÖ

"MOSTOFI", 14 YEARS, TAX COLLECTOR'S HEIR

Mirza Mohammad (ca 1896)

Amir Kabir, his minister, sought education for the country. He was murdered. The Shah preferred selling consessions to foreign firms.

MEANWHILE, THE COLONIAL POWERS DIVIDED THE WORLD:

Avantgarde, friends!

THE WHOLE WORLD ...?! NO! PERSIA HARVESTED THE FRUITS OF THE DAR AL-FONUM*:

Almost peaceful reform, thanks to parliament! Take that, world!

AHMAD, 12 YEARS SHAH-TO-BE

* HOUSE OF KNOWLEDGE, FOUNDED BY AMIR KABIR, 1851

LIKE A FAIRYTALE? 1925: BEGGAR BOY INSTEAD OF PRINCE

Reza Khan* Pahlavi becomes the new Shah!

*THE LONG-TIME DEFENSE MINISTER WAS NOT ALLOWED TO BE PRESIDENT

*FORMER FINANCIAL MINISTER

Without me*

Stripped of inherited privileges, Mohammad moves from Paris to Switzerland and earns a doctorate in inheritance law.

BACK IN TEHRAN: ... in 1952, Mohammad, now Prime Minister, writes to parliament:

To many dead politicians

Note:
○ **Persia needs political police force**
- Innocence? - **Out.**
- Reform opponents? - **Out.**
- Opponents of the Goverment?
○ Removed, even **with violence**

Us too ?

The history of the police in Iran goes back a long way

Me too?

No!

... and if you are not dead yet, find the rest on the net!

Check the Background:

- Who was Mohammad Mossadegh, and why is he such a central figure in Iran's history?

• What connections can you make between the comic and the history of Iran?

Who is Isnogud, and what are his goals?

_____
_____
_____
_____
_____
_____
_____
_____

Reflection:

• Why might the author have chosen this comic character to illustrate the theme of power in Iran? What does this say about the relationship between history and satire?

_____
_____
_____
_____
_____

• Can satire, as seen in this comic, help in understanding complex issues like abuse of power or political intrigue? Why or why not?

Discuss:

• What parallels can be drawn between Isnogud's behavior and the mechanisms of power and intrigue in reality?

• Why does the comic say, "Beggar boy instead of prince..."? Who was Reza Kahn Pahlavi before being appointed Shah by the parliament?

• How are political narratives created, and why are they so powerful?

• Create an additional panel for the comic: What might Isnogud experience in today's world? How would he navigate modern power structures or surveillance? Explain your design.

E) Breaking Free from the GDR:

A "Peaceful Revolution"?

• What does the word "revolution" mean? Does this term fit the events in the GDR? Are there alternative terms that better describe the change?

• What challenges did people in the GDR face, and how are they similar to struggles in other countries like Iran or places that went through big changes in society?

Check the Background:

• Research the "Monday Demonstrations" in Leipzig and other cities in the GDR. How did people manage to raise their voices despite fear and surveillance?

• What role did citizen movements, the church, or other independent groups play in this process?

1. Discuss:

• What impact did the UN Resolution 39/11 of 1984, which opposed inhumane border practices, have on the protest movement in the GDR? In what ways can the strategies and approaches of GDR citizens be compared to those of the anti-apartheid movement in South Africa — or not?

2. Creative Task:

• Write a fictional newspaper report about a Monday Demonstration from the perspective of a participant. Make sure to capture the emotions and thoughts of the people involved.

• Alternatively:

Imagine you are working for a radio station reporting live from the Berlin Wall in 1989. Prepare a short audio clip.

• Was the movement in the GDR truly "peaceful"? Where is it evident that violence and oppression had previously shaped people?

Reflect separately.

• What can we learn today from the peaceful movement in the GDR? In what way does it demonstrate that societal change is possible without violence?

Vocabulary Bank

• Add: Monday Demonstration, Stasi, opposition, reunification, transformation. Discuss slogans from the time, such as "We are the people," and reflect on their meaning and context.

Afsaneh
One from Many

This final chapter is designed to help you explore the overall structure

of Afsaneh - One from Many

The next pages allow you to dive into the following topics:

Self-Reflection:

 • What different types of texts have you discovered in the book (e.g. letter, dialogue, comic, reflection)?

• Why might these types have been intentionally chosen?
• How do these types of texts shape your reading experience and help you understand the themes?

Reflect separately.

A) The Conscious Use of Different Text Types

4. Afsaneh - One from Many .... entire Text

- Pick two different types of texts from the book and compare them.
- How does each text type make you feel or think?

TEXT A	TEXT B

Creative Task:

Imagine you need to convey a message from the book in a different type of text (e.g. a poem, a news story, or a monologue).

- How would you do it?

- Which type of text spoke to you the most? Why?

B) Afsaneh's Perspective:
A Universal Story?

• What parallels can you draw between Afsaneh's experiences and those of other people around the world?

• Are there universal themes that go beyond Afsaneh's deeply personal story?

Reflect separately.

Check the Background:

- Which texts are accessible to you that tell additional or different stories of women from Iran?
- Find reports from people who are experiencing similar struggles with cultural identity today. Whether through migration or political resistance, what connects their stories to Afsaneh's?

- Write a short text from the perspective of another character or person you imagine in the context of the book (or for example, a young woman in today's Iran):

- Is Afsaneh's story unique, or could she truly be "one from many"?
- Why?

- What values does the book share?
- What stylistic tools are used to express them?

VALUES	STYLISTIC TOOLS

Check the Background:

- Research the term "loss of values." What types of media publish reports on this topic?
- Which websites did you visit most often while working on *Afsaneh – One from Many*?
- Where can you find information for future questions?

- Which chapters or texts in *Afsaneh – One from Many* strongly emphasize messages about values?

Reflect separately.

1. Collect Quotes:
• Find quotes from the book that convey an important message to you. Discuss in small groups why these messages are relevant.

2. Creative Task:
• Choose three messages to summarize in a poster, graphic, or hashtag. How would it look?

• Which values or messages from the book would you adopt as guiding principles for yourself?
• Which ones wouldn't you, and why?

D) Visions for the Future
Iran and the World

"Our transitional generation has the opportunity to pause page 74
and fully utilize its capacity for reflection, in order to
prepare itself with all its resources for shaping the future."

Maryanne Wolf,

Proust and the Squid: The Story and Science of the Reading Brain, p. 268

The political situation in Iran has never been solely the page 21
concern of those whom the Greeks, after their conquest,
called Persians.

Reflection:

• Maryanne Wolf describes how books help us develop
our imagination and empathy.
What does this mean for your view of Iran and the world?

_____

_____

_____

_____

• What are your hopes for the future of Iran and other countries?
What role do tolerance, freedom, and education play in achieving
them?

_____

_____

_____

_____

1. Compare:

• Read the quote by Maryanne Wolf on page 74 carefully.

• What does she mean by the power of books to expand our imagination?

• How could this be significant for Iran?

2. Creative Task:

• Create a wish list or vision for the future of Iran or the world. Use terms and ideas from the book, such as "tolerance", "diversity" or "education".

• Do you believe that narratives and stories truly have the power to change the world? Why or why not?

• Check your Vocabulary Bank. Which terms will you use more often in the future?

Reflect separately.

Vocabulary Bank:

Here's your checklist:
Use this to mark which words you already know and make notes about the ones that are new or particularly interesting to you.

A broader vocabulary not only helps with reading and learning but also enables you to better understand the world and its topics. By becoming aware of their meanings, you develop a sense of how words and terms shape our thinking and our questions about life.

☐ Ahimsa (foreign word: nonviolence)

☐ accept

☐ adapt

☐ Army of Knowledge

☐ authoritarian

☐ break out

☐ breaking free

☐ challenge

☐ community

☐ critically

☐ culture

☐ culturally

☐ democracy

☐ describe

☐ dialog

☐ diaspora

☐ diplomatic

☐ discover

☐ discriminate

- ☐ discriminating
- ☐ diversity
- ☐ dynamic
- ☐ empathic
- ☐ freedom
- ☐ growth
- ☐ helpful
- ☐ hospitality
- ☐ identity
- ☐ inspiring
- ☐ Iranian
- ☐ justice
- ☐ learning
- ☐ literary
- ☐ migration
- ☐ narrative
- ☐ nation-state
- ☐ open
- ☐ open-mindedness
- ☐ peaceful
- ☐ Persian
- ☐ Persian poetry
- ☐ personally
- ☐ politically
- ☐ reflecting
- ☐ reflect
- ☐ sustainable

- [ ] sustainability
- [ ] solidarity
- [ ] supportive
- [ ] together
- [ ] transformation
- [ ] understanding
- [ ] value
- [ ] responsibility
- [ ] visualization
- [ ] visionary
- [ ] writing

- [ ]

- [ ]

- [ ]

- [ ]

- [ ]

- [ ]

- [ ]

- [ ]

☐

☐

☐

☐

☐

☐

☐

☐

☐

☐

☐

☐

☐

□

□

□

□

□

□

□

□

□

□

□

□

□

□

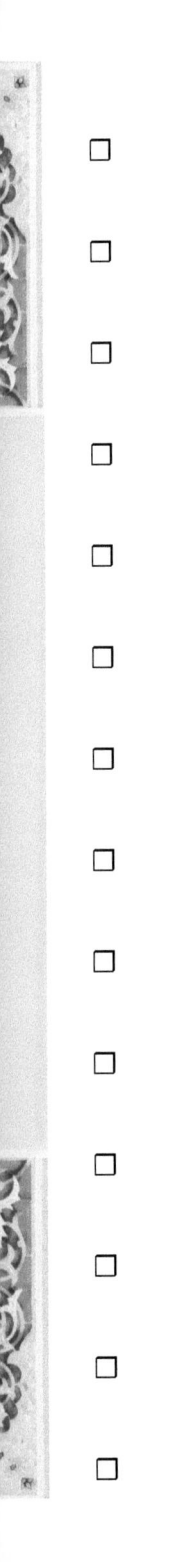

☐

☐

☐

☐

☐

☐

☐

☐

☐

☐

☐

☐

☐

Tips for Educators:

An exciting journey lies ahead as you guide curious minds along their path.

By carefully selecting the exercises, you can tailor your approach to your group of learners, sparking both curiosity and a spirit of exploration.

Expanding Language Together:

Project Vocabulary Bank

This is not just a tool for collecting words but a collaborative project that promotes learning and exchange.

Through interactive exercises, regular reflection, and integration into lessons, you can create a dynamic language-learning environment that motivates and inspires students.

Aims:
• Encourage active and creative engagement with new terms.
• Help students use the Vocabulary Bank as a dynamic and collaborative tool.
• Create an environment where vocabulary is continuously expanded and applied.

Introduction:
Explain the Vocabulary Bank as a "living document".
• Emphasize that it is shaped by the entire group and constantly evolving.
• Introduce the different functions of the Vocabulary Bank: collecting, understanding, and applying.
• Discuss the pros and cons of the media or tools the group wants to use.

Jenseits von richtig und falsch
da treffen wir uns •Rumi

Digital:
Use cloud services such as Google Docs, Padlet, or school platforms. This allows collaborative work in real time.

Analog:
Use posters, pinboards, or a large notebook placed in the classroom.

Develop a Roadmap Together:
• Work collaboratively to establish a plan for helping students build and maintain the Vocabulary Bank.
• Start by creating an initial list of words from the book as a group.
Decide which information to collect for each word (e.g. definition, synonyms, example sentences, translations).

Rotating Responsibility:

Assign a small group each week to add new words from the current chapter to the Vocabulary Bank.

Learning Through Games and Quizzes:
• Create quiz questions from the Vocabulary Bank, such as guessing definitions or spelling words.
• Use digital tools like Kahoot! for fun and interactive quizzes.

This approach allows for both individual and collaborative engagement.

Homework:
• Have students use words from the Vocabulary Bank in their own sentences.

Team Challenges:
• Who can creatively incorporate the most words into a story or poem?

Regular Reflection and Application:
At the end of each chapter, the class can discuss and highlight the most important terms in a vocabulary round.

• Ask: Which word was the most difficult? Which one did you find particularly interesting?
• Encourage students to use words from the Vocabulary Bank in creative projects or discussions.
• Connect words to current topics or personal experiences.

Long-Term Integration and Connection to the Book:

• Continuously incorporate the Vocabulary Bank into work with the chapters.
• Check if the words are being actively used in tasks and discussions.

Continuous Maintenance:
• Encourage students to keep using and expanding the Vocabulary Bank even after completing the workbook.

• Lead by example and develop your own Ideas:

Reflect separately.

1. A) The Letter: Introduction and Intercultural Reflection

Afsaneh's letter serves as a tool for intercultural learning and personal reflection. Its direct address to the students makes Afsaneh's story more accessible and provides an interactive and emotional introduction to the workbook.

1. B) *Woman - Life - Freedom*: A Global Movement

This contemporary connection encourages students to research sociopolitical topics. This unit links the universal values of freedom and equality to a real, ongoing movement. Learners are invited to reflect on these themes and engage with them creatively. Empathy, intercultural understanding, and the ability to form independent opinions are nurtured.

1. C) Iran and the United Nations

The historical perspective on Iran's active role in global politics develops research skills and an understanding of international cooperation. The ability to connect global issues to personal values fosters curiosity about how political decisions have long-term impacts.

1. D) Rumi - The Persian Poet and Philosopher

Discovering Rumi's messages and applying them to the challenges of today's world offers not only an introduction to Persian poetry but also an opportunity to reflect on universal values such as humanity, love, and community.

2. My Notes - Section II

2. A) Youth under Fascism: Responsibility and Compassion

Learners are encouraged to critically engage with history, responsibility, and their own perspectives.
The following discussions require thoughtful facilitation:
• Can young people be held accountable for their decisions in totalitarian regimes?
• What could help young people today avoid making similar mistakes?

2. B) Boundaries: Urban Societies and Nations

Using boundaries as a metaphor for societal division opens up a field for multidimensional thinking and discussion.

It is helpful to connect historical events:

• Use the topic of boundaries as a starting point to draw parallels between the emergence of urban societies, the formation of nation-states, and the division of Germany.
• Emphasize that boundaries are not just physical lines but can also create social, cultural, and psychological barriers.

Emotional Connection:

• Share vivid stories of how people on both sides of a boundary experience life.
For example, let students hear reports of families separated by the Berlin Wall or individuals who overcame city walls to gain freedom. This makes history tangible and emotionally relatable.

Boundaries as a Mirror of the Present:

• Discuss with students how boundaries function today, such as within the EU, along refugee routes, or in digital communities.

• Explore how the world has changed since the adoption of UN Resolution 39/11 in 1984, which is said to have influenced measures like dismantling landmines and self-firing devices in the GDR's "death strip" along the western border.

Interactive Exercise on the Berlin Wall:

• Have the class create a symbolic boundary in the classroom (e.g. with tape) and assign different rights to the resulting groups.

• Discuss how the separated groups feel on each side. Use this as a starting point to talk about Germany's division and draw parallels to other historical or contemporary boundaries.

Parallels to Afsaneh's Experiences:

• Highlight how boundaries played a role in Afsaneh's life — whether through the cultural and political barriers *between East and West* or through personal limits she had to overcome.

• Discuss: What "boundaries" did Afsaneh have to overcome through her emigration, and how did this shape her and her identity?

Engaging Students Actively:

• Encourage students to share their own experiences with "boundaries" — whether geographical, social, or emotional. Personal connections foster a deeper understanding of how boundaries impact lives.

Dividing Tasks:

• Divide the class into groups to explore different aspects of boundaries (e.g. historical city boundaries, national borders, virtual boundaries in the digital world).
Have each group present their findings to create a diverse perspective.
Provide space for students to investigate how UN Resolution 39/11 has impacted global mobility and the movement of people.

Developing Future Perspectives:

• Discuss what the world might look like without boundaries. Encourage a critical discussion about the pros and cons of openness versus limitation to conclude the topic.

• By connecting the discussion to the present and the students' personal experiences, this creates an engaging and meaningful exploration of the importance of boundaries.

2. C) The Power of Language: Words Shape Worlds

These tasks invite learners to critically question the power of language and use it as a tool for positive change.

 Initial experiences with their own Vocabulary Bank have been collected. Help the students organize the Vocabulary Bank together as a *living document*.

Sensitivity in Addressing Political Topics:

This topic is highly sensitive, as it involves the suppression of human rights and freedom of speech.

Foster an open mindset and emphasize that students' opinions are valuable. Encourage critical thinking without pressuring them to adopt a "correct" opinion.

Connecting to Personal Realities:

• Draw parallels to examples from other countries or students' everyday lives. Show how language holds power, even in social media or school environments.
Ask: Have you ever experienced how words can hurt or help?

Empowerment through Language:

• Focus on helping students understand how they can use language positively — to express themselves, to connect with others, or to stand up for justice.

Promoting Media Skills:

• Have students research how language is used in media to influence opinions. Critically discuss how they can navigate and respond to such mechanisms.

* HOUSE OF KNOWLEDGE, FOUNDED BY AMIR KABIR, 1851

2. D) Prosperity through Sustainable Management

This task combines historical research with current questions about sustainability, highlighting the importance of wise resource management — both in the past and today.

Connecting History and the Present:

• Show students that sustainable resource management is not just a historical issue but also a solution to today's challenges, such as climate change and food security.

Developing Research Skills:

Encourage students to find trustworthy online sources and approach information critically.
• Provide tips on reliable websites (e.g. LeMO, UNESCO, anthropological institutes, or scientific articles).

Interdisciplinary Approaches:

• Link the topic to geography, history, and biology to give students a more comprehensive understanding.

 Let students work together in groups to present their findings and draw conclusions.

3. Our Dialogue - Section III-IV .... Pages 28-75

3. A) The Army of Knowledge: Revolution through Education

Recognizing the importance of education for a society's progress and how initiatives like the "Army of Knowledge" can lay the foundation for sustainable development gives students space to explore their own ideas of shared responsibility.
At the same time, they should be encouraged to critically examine the contradictions and challenges of such a "system".

Background:
Explore how education was one of the central themes of the "White Revolution". The "Army of Knowledge" was an initiative aimed at providing young people in rural areas with access to basic education and was recognized by UNESCO for its efforts.

• Use maps and statistics to highlight the rural regions of Iran where literacy rates were particularly low.

• **Point out that education is a privilege that is not equally accessible in all countries.**

3. B) Fairy Tales: Tales that Travel

Recognize fairy tales as a global phenomenon that connects people across generations and cultures: Students should critically examine the origins and transformations of stories while reflecting on stereotypes.

Background:
• Clarify that many fairy tales considered national often originate from stories in other cultures.
• Explain how fairy tales developed through oral traditions, travel, and literary adaptations. Provide examples from different regions to highlight diversity and cultural exchange.

Emphasize that fairy tales do not have fixed cultural boundaries but grow through exchange and adaptation.
Avoid assigning fairy tales exclusively to specific nationalities or cultures, and instead promote an open perspective.

• Use maps or timelines to trace the journey of fairy tales. Encourage students to get creative by retelling stories from their own region or culture, helping them understand the process of cultural exchange.

3. C) Farah Diba:
Between Hard Work and Representation

Different Perceptions:

• Discuss with the group why Farah Diba is perceived differently in various societies: as a representative of a modern Iran or as a symbol of the upper class.

Not a Fairy Tale, but Reality:

• Emphasize the hard work and responsibility that came with Farah Diba's role.

• Encourage students to critically question whether and how these duties are carried out today by monarchs, influencers, or other representatives.

Connecting Point Fairy Tales:

• Build on the discussion about fairy tales from point B.

• Ask: How does the life of a monarch like Farah Diba differ from the world of fairy tales? Which values from fairy tales (e.g. justice, beauty, courage) might have been reflected in her actions?

3. D) "Unriddle the Comic": Power and Intrigue

• **Provide Context:**

 Briefly explain who Mohammad Mossadegh was without presenting a fixed opinion.
Encourage students to explore for themselves why he is evaluated so differently.

 Emphasize that there are many perspectives on history. Encourage critical thinking and a willingness to confront uncomfortable truths.

Ensure that students understand how political narratives are created and why they are so powerful.
This is especially important as they make their own connections between the past and the present.

3. E) Breakting Free from the GDR: A "Peaceful Revolution"?

Question the Term "Revolution":

• Discuss with students whether the term "revolution" is appropriate for the GDR movement, or if other terms, such as "transformation" or "peaceful change", might be more fitting.

Building Bridges:

• Draw parallels to other peaceful movements worldwide and explore why some succeeded while others did not.

Fostering Empathy:

• Use creative tasks to help students imagine what it might have felt like to be part of such a movement. This makes history more tangible and highlights its connection to the present.

4. Afsaneh – One from Many .... entire Text

How can Afsaneh's personal story help address themes like identity, migration, and cultural diversity in the classroom?
Which of the values discussed in the book would you like to emphasize most?

4. A) The Conscious Use of Different Text Types

• Develop students' ability to recognize different types of texts and analyze their impact.

- Encourage creative thinking by expressing content in various formats.

Guidelines for Implementation:
- Start with a brief introduction to text types (e.g. letters, dialogues, comics) and their functions.
- Use examples from the book to highlight how stylistic devices like humor, emotionality, or reflection influence the reader.
- Discuss how the choice of text type impacts readability and messaging.

- Encourage small group work to promote diverse perspectives and ideas.
- Ensure the creative task is open-ended to allow for individual strengths and interests to shine.

4. B) Afsaneh's Perspective: A Universal Story?

- Discuss how Afsaneh's story can be both unique and representative at the same time.

- Foster empathy through perspective shifts and engagement with parallel life experiences.

- Connect Afsaneh's story to current global issues.

- Encourage the group to use a variety of sources for their research, such as news articles, videos, or interviews.

- Allow students to bring in their personal experiences or those of people from their community to enrich the discussion.

- Offer the option to approach the perspective-shifting task artistically (e.g. through drawings, poems, or monologues).

4. C) Values and Messages of the Book

• What values does the text convey (e.g. tolerance, respect, freedom)? Identify quotes that reflect these values for your work. In which chapters or texts do you find these messages?

4. D) Visions for the Future - Iran and the World

Foster a respectful atmosphere where all opinions and ideas are welcome.

• This topic invites students to develop their own vision for the future while reflecting on the role of literature and education in societal transformation.

• Further questions: What specific changes or improvements do students wish for in their own environment? How can they personally contribute to making these aspirations a reality?

No Reading Journal,
but an invitation
to collect your impressions
while working with the text:

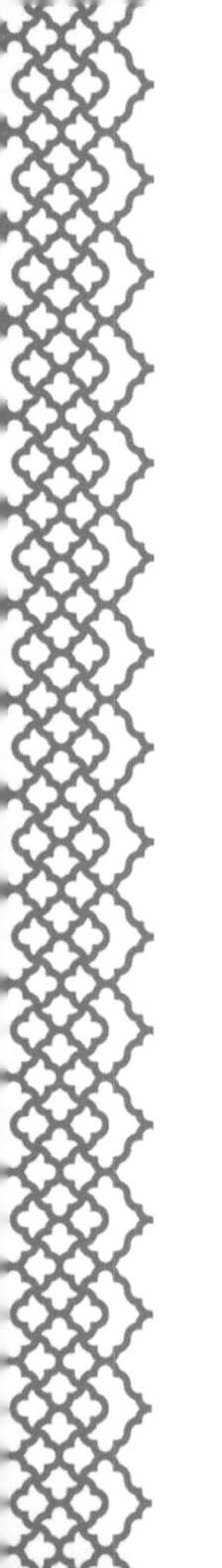

more keywords ...

References and Recommended Resources:

Dr. Parnaz Kianiparsa & Dr. Sara Vali: Bā ham A1. Persisch für Anfänger, Ernst Klett Sprachen, Stuttgart 2018.

Maulana Dschelaladdin Rumi: Von Allem und vom Einen, übers. Annemarie Schimmel, Diederichs Verlag, München 2020.

Rashin Kheiriyeh: Rumi. Dichter der Liebe, übers. Thomas Bodmer, NordSüd Verlag, Zürich 2023.

Stephan Orth, Samuel Zuder, Mina Esfandiari: Iran. Tausend und ein Widerspruch, National Geographic, München 2018.

Cornelius Adebahr: Inside Iran. Alte Nation, neue Macht?, Dietz, Bonn 2018.

Geschichte der Welt. Eine Jahreschronik in Daten, Fakten und Bildern, Dorling Kindersley, München 2012.

Barnabas & Anabel Kindersley: Kinder aus aller Welt, übers. Anne Braun, Loewe, Bindlach 1997.

Marshall B. Rosenberg: Gewaltfreie Kommunikation, Junfermann, Paderborn 2003.

Maryanne Wolf: Das lesende Gehirn. Wie der Mensch zum Lesen kam - und was es in unseren Köpfen bewirkt, Spektrum, Heidelberg 2009.

Geo Epoche Kollektion: Der Nahe Osten. Vom 15. Jahrhundert bis heute: Die Geschichte einer umkämpften Region, Heft Nr. 30, Hamburg 2023.

Geo Epoche - Das Magazin für Geschichte: Das alte Persien. Die Geschichte eines Weltreichs - von der Antike bis zur Blüte unter den Muslimen. 550 v. Chr. - 1722 n. Chr., Heft Nr. 99, Hamburg 2019.

Geo Epoche - Das Magazin für Geschichte: Das Osmanische Reich 1300-1922, Heft Nr. 56, Hamburg 2012.

Isnogud. Der Großwesir. Die Goscinny- & Tabary-Jahre 1962-1969, Carlsen Comics, Hamburg 2023.

https://de.wikipedia.org/wiki/Liste_persischer_Erfinder_und_Entdecker
https://de.wikipedia.org/wiki/Persischer_Korridor
https://www.un.org/en/
https://www.nobelpeaceprize.org
https://www.iranicaonline.org

Afsaneh, like the author, are literary figures who emerged from countless conversations with women rich in life experience, coming together to offer all readers and young people insights into the facts, feelings, and thoughts of those who live in Germany today.

Vera Ansén

* 1972, was born in Wiesbaden and grew up in Cologne. She studied theater, film, and television studies, pedagogy, philosophy, and even psychology? She still believes that the head is round so that thoughts can circulate more freely.
With her many talents in words and images, she helps others overcome their speechlessness and never forgets: to entertain well!
Stay curious!

This Workbook

accompanies

Afsaneh ~ One from Many

and is available wherever

books are sold!

ISBN 978-3-769-31572-1

Afsaneh is from Iran, I am from Germany.
Is that enough for us to write a book?

Our dialogue grew from so many questions:
about her homeland, life, and the future
she seeks for her granddaughter.

Maybe not everything written in this book
is true. But one way or another, that's
probably how it happened. The rest you'll
find online, the beginning here ...